Chivalry
and
Malevolence

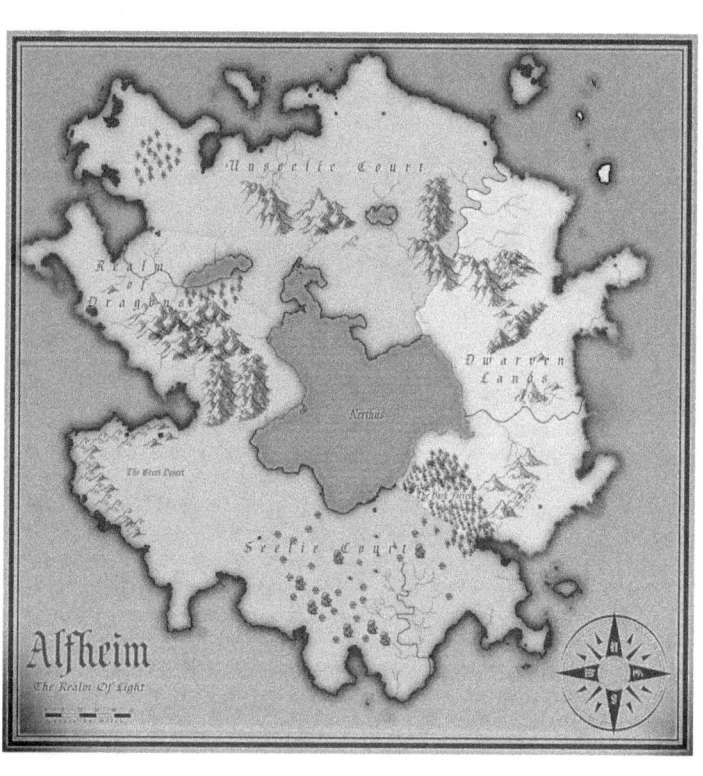

Alfheim

The Realm Of Light

Chivalry
and
Malevolence

A Nine Realms Tale

RAE Z. RYANS

Published 2013 By Fictitious Publishing an imprint of Viciously Fictitious Media Productions
www.viciouslyfictitious.com

Chivalry and Malevolence: A Nine Realms Tale
ISBN 978-0615775098
www.raezryans.com

Cover and interior design: Raven Tree Design
www.raventreedesign.com

Contents

Chapter One
The Dreadful Princess

It was blissfully cold for a summer day. One could breathe and watch their breath dance in the sunlight. Snow covered the ground, but that was nothing new. There was always snow or ice in Alfheim.

My fingers drummed, as I awaited the courier sending news from the neighboring kingdom, the realm of the dragon. The desolate land also served as home to my intended. How absurd for an elf to marry a dragon, but alas the announcement would spread across the kingdoms in the coming days.

This was not the word I awaited, no, there was excitement brewing on the horizon. Today marked more than battle and marriage. I grew tired of the war, endless conflict fought in the names of Gods whom had long forgotten their people. We were not people or human. I laughed to even call ourselves that. No, we were the Light Elves and Faeries of Alfheim.

This was a forbidden realm where man had never walked before; they had not yet spread the pollution of their words or actions. That all ended now, as the wards, the magic of my people, all of it failed.

Today a portal appeared in the eastern kingdom of Ironwood. A man arrived from another world, the whispers of the servants told me. Father sent his sentries out to capture him, and seal the anomaly off for good.

I shook my finger and mimicked his words. "The realm of light should remain closed as the Greater Faerie King mandated. Men could not be trusted with magic." This realm bore it to the races of Faerie, their cousins the Elves, the Dragon, and even some of the minor races had traces of the Myst.

Not I, not even for an elf, did the MystMyst flow through my veins. Mother claimed it was a weakness and not becoming of my station. Nobility bred strong mages, shamans, and to a lesser extent those with the ability to mend another person. In many ways, I was just like the human who crossed into our realm. I was worthless, but deemed not a threat.

"My lady, where are you? The Queen has summoned you," my lady in waiting shouted into my rooms. She could say or do nothing to make me want to meet with my mother. I was her daughter when it became convenient to her. There was no love between us, not like I had any real notion of love.

"I am here." My voice was softer than I had expected, yet I did not move. My eyes bore out into the distance. There, not more than a few miles out, I caught the lavender banner of my people approaching the castle. Reaching into my cloak, I withdrew my spyglass for a closer look.

At first, all I saw were the warrior elves and dwarfs. As they drew nearer, a magnificent beast akin to our dear Pegasus trotted into view. I could not gauge the size from my distance, but the black coat glistened in the sunlight, as it trekked through the snowdrifts. Atop the creature was a man, made of silver. I blinked and peered through the glass again. He glinted like a shining star in the darkness.

This human must be a fine warrior to wear such equipment on his body. Ours wore far less into battles. Then again, the people here relied heavily on magic, and not so much upon their brute strength. The shame of it weighed on my shoulders. My people would find themselves lost if their Myst waned as mine did.

"Princess Morgana, please we mustn't keep the Queen waiting," the maid whined and grasped my arm, dragging me from watching the glorious sight.

"What is it she wants of me today?" One could never tell. I knew of course, mother wanted to speak of my betrothal to the Prince Drust of Durkheim. If I actually had a say in the matter, I would have told her no.

The match was not as imperfect as it was impossible. Drust was a dragon who wielded powerful magic. He even took on the form of an elf, but he could take the form of any creature that breathed. He was kind and sweet, but the union was not out of love. The Prince wished to save me from my family, but dragons held clutches of wives and consorts. Even if love did eventually bloom, I would never be the only one, nor could I ask it of him.

Every woman held dreams of love. That fantasy, I gave up long ago. At nineteen, no one offered anything to me. I could not blame them. After all, who wanted to marry the shrouded elf, with rumors of ugly scars beneath her veils? No, there were no hard feelings held against the fine Princes and royalty of the realm.

That left my final hope in the hands of my savior and friend. My father and brother, agreed with Drust's proposal. The two families spent the past year ironing out all the details of my dowry.

Of course, that left me at the mercy of my mother. I swore she wished to see me gone, and not in the betrothed way. I asked father about her behavior once, but he pushed it aside. Not once did he question the veils I wore to cover the majority of my face. In Alfheim, men did not rule or create the laws. They enforced them and fought.

"Prince Drust is arriving tomorrow." I rolled my eyes, as Georgiana pulled the clean, royal blue gown over my head. I hated to wear dresses, and often wished I were born a man. The men had it so much easier. There was little need for layer upon layer, the pinning of sleeves, and who could forget the breath-stealing corset.

My arms spread wide, as she donned the final changes. As a child, I often pretended they were the wings of a dragon. Now that I would soon be engaged to one, it no longer seemed fun. In secret, I still coveted the power. It was akin to what one felt as they fell in a dream. Your stomach reeled in a humorous way as if you did an extraordinary thing.

Never could I understand why women bothered primping. None of it mattered, especially not for me. The deep gashes etched in my face were all that mattered to the outsiders. Even those within my court never saw the damage. Mother forbade it; she made me hide it since my magic failed to heal it. Part of me was glad. It served as a reminder of my inner strength.

"Have you heard anything about the man that they caught?" If it was he atop the beast then he certainly wore odd clothing. My people wore fitted, but simple and elegant garments made of soft, silky material from the enchanted worms. The flashiness appeared only in the color, and adornments were scarcely used even by the royal Unseelie courts. Such distaste, as mother often said, was for the remainder of the Nine Realms.

"You should not speak of such things, my lady." The younger woman let out a breath. I knew she could get into trouble if she told me. She knew something about the man in the shining suit of metal. The state of her chewed lip gave her away.

The idea of the stranger intrigued me. It excited the bumbles in my belly, and my curiosity could not be satiated, until I learned everything about him.

"I apologize Georgiana. It must be the anticipation of the impending betrothal. Prince Drust hasn't even officially asked me yet," I lied. There was no excitement at all. I did not want to become the Princess of Durkheim. Not in this world, not a part of this court, all of it left me queasy.

"How shall you wear your hair today, my lady?" I bit my tongue. Why must I go through this every single day? The maid knew the Queen allowed it worn one way.

It was times such as this that I wished I had been born with more magic. Ok, so it was on my mind all the time. All the other elves in my kingdom appeared more adept to the arts. No, the Gods did not smile upon me, when I was born into the world. First, they cursed me as a woman. The second was no ability whatsoever other than my sharp mind and tongue. Mother longed to rid herself of me. She told me as daily. My brow cocked. Perhaps she thought Drust would show cruelty as she did to me.

"The same as always. It matters little to me, yet you waste my time in asking," I muttered under my breath. Her pale cheeks colored; she heard every word. Swiftly she braided and wrapped my midnight hair into a tight bun. Georgiana attached the veil last, with a lovely comb of abalone shell. I made it myself. One of my many possessions with a fond memory attached.

Once dressed and primped, the guard escorted me to mother's sitting room. The air chilled with her presence, and I shuddered. Dread set in, but I forced it down. I could not afford to show weakness. She always took advantage of it. Every time the malevolent beast awakened within the Queen, it seethed to hook its tendrils into me.

My eyes dropped to my skirts, and I placed my hands behind my back. She was above me, and it was disrespectful otherwise. Mother neither arose nor acknowledged my entrance. The clock ticked on the stone mantle. Patiently I waited until she motioned for me to sit. I grew tired of the regales she demanded. She claimed it a learning experience, but it was a boorish nightmare. In many ways, the thought of a, freedom with Drust appealed to me. If only it could happen the way I envisioned it, how every girl did. Cloaked in white, and a happily ever after, but I was foolish to believe in faerie tales.

Silence remained between us, as she stared me up and down. The gaze cut right through me, the tingle of her power rolled over my skin. She sought flaws, anything to ridicule me further. My breathing her air alone was enough to set her off, but alas, she summoned me. That should count in my favor, but I was not lucky.

An eternity passed between us, sitting idly as if we awaited some drastic news. I wished to be anywhere else. A land where the sun shined giving a false sense of happiness. From the southern kingdoms of my cousin, I heard tales of rain, water pelting from the sky and green grasses. She even spoke of flowers fragrant and bright. I sighed inward, wishing to visit her lands.

"No man wants a day dreaming twit for a wife." Mother's voice was cold enough to cut through the ice. My hands grew restless and damp wondering, nay, praying words would remain her weapon today. Her words were the only weapon left that did not scar me.

Strange distant sounds hit my ears: clip, clop, clip, clop. My heart raced in anticipation. I had never heard a noise like it before. Metal against stone. The prisoner, it was the man who appeared out of thin air through the rift. I was sure of it.

"Sorry Mother, I shall try to stop those tendencies." Her eyes darkened. It was as if I unleashed a storm within her. I swallowed hard and glanced to my hands. One she only released toward me. My hands trembled as her magic took hold, choking the air from my lungs. I cursed the Gods and closed my eyes.

"Mother," my brother said. My lids fluttered open for a moment. Brennus barged through the door. His tall lanky frame, the perfect build for an elf, rushed to my aid. He always saved me when he able. Luckily for him, those days would end soon.

My head lulled to the side, as he carried me from her chambers, and out into the brisk air. Although the pain was still great, my senses returned. Mother's power only reached so far, and she did not follow.

The sound of the man grew closer, but I was not prepared to lay eyes upon the beast. Nothing would have prepared me for the vision of the shinning man. My mouth dropped open. Both were beyond my vocabulary and comprehension.

"Princess Morgana, you should not be outside," my personal guard Lotho scolded. If he had any idea what I escaped from, his words would not cut me. Very few knew of the abuses their Queen inflicted upon her daughter, the Princess.

"This is the man? What is this glorious beast he rides upon?" The creature snorted, and its legs danced. The man said nothing. His face covered by the metal, but his hands were bound to the beast by what appeared as leather thongs.

"The Princess asked you a question." Lotho turned his attention to the man, giving him a shove for good measure. The beast reared, and a shriek left its mouth. Perhaps it was mine, as I scrambled from my brother's arms. The silver clad man toppled off; his helm rattled along the stones. He was handsome.

"My Lord, are you alright?" I ran to his side not knowing if he survived the fall. My people were not immortal, not as other legends boasted, but who knew about humans. Much was unknown about the young race, and perhaps they held secrets we did not know.

"Princess, please back away from him right now," Lotho or Brennus shouted. I could not tell which yelled.

"No, he may need help," I muttered, as Lotho and Brennus tried to pry me from his side. There was blood. Crimson dripped from his forehead, and the man did not open his eyes. The man was young, not many lines crossed his features. The hair upon his head and face were a lovely, earthy brown and cropped short against his head. The ears were odd. They did not end with a point. Instead, they curved back toward the head.

"Princess, I beg you to please step away from the prisoner." Prisoner? Why would they consider this man as such an atrocity? What crime did he commit? I wanted to ask, but I knew such matters would never reach my ears. After all, I was a woman. Brute force and enforcement were for the men.

I allowed the magic, what little essence I possessed, to flow to my fingertips. The green Myst escaped, binding into the cut of the man's skin. It weaved into his body, and tiny creatures erupted, sewing the skin anew. When the deed was completed, the magic returned to the ground.

"Take him to the prison," Lotho commanded his officers, as he grabbed me, and held me back.

"It iss not becoming of a Princessss to touch another man. Prince Durssst would be disssspleased to know about the humansss," the guard hissed his warning in my ear. It told me why, unexpectedly, I had received my own guard. My eyes narrowed, and I crossed my arms over my chest. Dragon or not, Lotho had no right to speak to me in a crude manner.

Throwing my nose in the air, I departed. *Drust would never know*, I thought. Besides, I was curious. It was not as if I wanted to run away with the strange creature. A smile spread over my face. That too was a faerie tale.

A piece of me expected an automatic hatred. After all, fondness towards humans was not an Unseelie trait. Today marked the first time I saw one outside of a book. We did not live amongst them, as others did in their home realm of Midgard. Alfheim remained one of the few closed to humans.

Still I could not stop thinking of him, as I paced about my rooms. I returned to my window, noting the guard remained in the courtyard below. They yelled and cursed at the man. No, I thought to myself. Human or not, this was not right. Just because he was different, unwanted even, they punished him. Was he any different from me?

I decided right then, I would do all in my power to save him. I knew that by doing this act of good I would put my own life in great risk, but what was a life of pain? What my family planned was cruel, violent, and bloody. Well known for their public executions, The Unseelie Court of Alfheim hated imperfection. The chaos fed their Myst; it was the Unseelie way, but it was not my way. There was also the beast, the wingless, black Pegasus. Must it die too?

I hoped that with any luck, the man held the power to return home. There was nowhere but the Seelie Court where he would find safety. Travel there took weeks without the Myst. Cursing drew my attention back to the window, and I stepped out onto the balcony. My guard exchanged words with my brother. He must have sensed my presence, as his gaze flickered to me. His yellowing eyes told me not to try anything foolish. They accused me, judged me, just like all the others. The way his stare raked over me made me shudder. The longer he stared, my skin slimed like the murky bogs in the south.

"Milady, supper will be soon," the annoyance rang clear in Georgiana's voice.

"I'll be right there." Such a foolish notion, getting dressed … ah that was it. My fingers snapped and a smile spread over my lips. A plan formed within my mind. There was a way to save the man and set him free. He stood a chance if I could free him of these walls.

"On second thought, Georgiana, I am feeling a bit peekish. I think it best to supper in my room." I tossed myself on the chaise and draped my arm over my head.

"The Queen-" No, I could not let her bully me any longer. This was the right thing to do. I forced a frown and groaned, clutching my middle, as her steps neared.

"Mother will understand. I am overwhelmed with Prince Drust's impending visit. You tell her those exact words. Tell her I seek to feel and look my best for him." She did not argue, and I did not care if she believed the folly. This gave me leave to wander during supper.

Georgiana would not return, and if by chance she did, I would set my rooms in farce. I could watch where they kept the man and his beast, and gather supplies. After everyone fell asleep, when the coast cleared during the nightly rotation of the royal guard, I would free him. The silver-clad man deserved as much.

Chapter Two
The Knight

Desperately, I sought my bearings. My hand touched against cold stone. Prison, was what the tall man said. At least there was one notion our worlds held in common. Wandering into a strange land had a way of doing that. I traveled home, to my king when I transported to this desolate, frozen place. It took only moments of the biting cold to have me wishing for the English summer, I left behind. Instead, I traded my home for a cell and my honored status for the term prisoner.

At first, I thought it was all a dream. I fell asleep atop my beloved Achilles whilst traveling. Even the people here appeared dreamlike. They were long and lean, perfection in their looks, but with deadly purple and yellow eyes. There were the smaller folks too, sturdy little men with axes. They were quick, agile, and lethal with their weapons. But this world was not a dream. Those peculiar people surrounded me, prodded me, and then they locked me away.

Did they hold magic to insert images, memories into my head? No, that was absurd … blasphemy even, but I could not deny, this place was not the same as my home. I shook my head of such traitorous thoughts. England, oh how I never thought I would miss the rolling countryside, the lush forests teaming with game, and ale. My throat burned in memory, of the bittersweet lager, as it slid down my aching throat after a day on the battlefield.

The notion of it did little to lighten me. The covered woman accomplished that. She marked the only gentle creature I met, in this foul new world. There was a beauty in that, and it made me wonder what lay beneath her coverings.

"Sheer desperation of a maddened man," I scolded myself aloud and ran my hand over my overgrown face. Even as a free man, it could not occur. I was a Knight, and that gave me no right to royalty in this land or at home.

Princess Morgana, the man called her. A smile overtook my face, and my heart hammered in remembrance. She appeared shorter; more of my own height than the males, but she held a gentle grace about her stature. A mystery lay beneath her covered features. I said nothing of it not wanting to make a scene, and knowing it was not my place. Did they hide away her astounding beauty? Curiosity, but what else would I think about to pass the time.

I sighed. It was not my place to note the strange features of others, but while I was pondering … the one male guard. There was something about him that felt inhuman. I laughed; nothing here looked human. The eyes were akin to the lizards my regime encountered in the dessert. Reptilian in appearance and sound. The scars covering his body lent me little relief. I too, wore the scars of battle, yet these were different. It was like they were a living, breathing piece of him. I shuddered; they were like scales. No, I would not spend my last hours or days thinking of the ghastly man.

"Lord, please guide me through these troubled times and bless the lady who aided me."

The Princess, when she spoke the sound hypnotized me, akin to a siren at sea. Like the voices upon the water, which led you to death. She resembled a dream. When I saw the princess and when she spoke, I awaited my death. The way she treated me with respect and curiosity moved me in that dire time. It was as if our roles reversed. Chivalry was not beneath her, not as it was at home.

Her kindness stunned me into utter silence and admiration. No, not a dream or fantasy, I reminded myself. Even with myself captured, hands bound to Achilles, I thought to wake myself. Instead, I accidentally pinched my mount. The well-worn charger bucked. I fell and realized the truth.

Pain screamed through my limbs. Blood poured from gashes left by my clattering helm. The Princess yelled at someone. Darkness came and I hated it. I did not want to miss a moment of her beauty, or the softness of her voice ringing like a fine harp in my ears. The Princess became my light in that cold, outlandish world, and I prayed for her, I prayed for me, as the grace of her voice faded.

I awoke in a room, my armor removed. A cell became my new home. In my slumber, someone redressed me. I glanced down at the ridiculous clothing. Even with the strange garments covering my body, I felt naked as a newborn babe. Tunic, pants, and odd shoes were thrusted upon my body. The colors were beyond absurd for any class of man, let alone a Knight. Whoever felt canary yellow and light blue a suitable color should be tarred and feathered.

I no longer had the protection of my plate. In this land, it left me exposed. My weapons were missing too. The sword that the King of England gifted to me was gone. My dagger that I kept in my saddle and all my provisions vanished. I had nothing left of my world but my thoughts, and even they seemed faded in comparison to the Princess.

If it was my world, negotiations would commence for my ransom. This was not the case. I doubted their plans. They would not release me except by pain of death. The reptilian man whispered as much to the other man. I wanted to die in battle or at the least within my world. This land already went beyond every belief I held true and dear.

Blasphemy … it echoed within the confines of my mind.

I sat up, noticing the simplicity of my cell. There were no outside windows in the space. This left me with no notion of the time that passed, however the temperature grew colder. Perhaps that was just the impending doom within the prison of my mind. Thick frigid walls surrounded me, with naught but a barred window in the door.

Laughter echoed and I realized it was my own. I stood and regretted the motion. Nausea rippled through my stomach, and pain seared my vision into a swirl of white dots. The fall affected me more than I realized. The fall ... how had I survived it? Running my hands over my head, I felt naught even a scratch. Surely, I remembered blood, my blood. The taste, it had trickled into my mouth.

A soft creak drew my attention. Footsteps approached, metal jingled, but I could not focus upon anything or anyone. The door swung open, and warmth settled over my weary body. A sweet, floral smell that I could not place wafted into my nostrils. A woman, it told me, but she spoke no words.

Fabric, rougher than my two days growth, fell over my head. It was not necessary, as I still could not see. Hands grabbed my arms, dragging me to my feet, and her smell grew stronger. I tried my best to hold steady, but I lost my footing. Still she did not speak.

Just as I righted myself, I felt the push of a strong arm in my back. My brow rose; perhaps I was wrong. Panic set in and my chest ached. Was this my glorious end? Years spent upon bloodied battlefields, fighting foes in the name of my King, and here I shall die a helpless chap.

I would die a shameful death in a distant land. There would be no great songs, no lavish feast to honor the passing of *Sir Thomas Graftfield*. I did not speak to my captor. To make a scene now would ensure any memory draped in cowardice. *I was not a coward*. My shoulders tightened and my back straightened. No, I was a Knight, and I refused to hang my head in shame. Then everything changed.

Cold air bit at me, and the scent of horses filled my nose, replacing the sweet smell of my guard. There was something more. Underneath it all, the mood changed with the shift of the wind. The hands upon my body grew lax, soft even. The only softness I knew in this land was that of the Princess. A man could dream, and imaginably that was what this truly was. A dream come true and I would hold it forever.

"You will have to pull yourself atop the beast, my Lord. I fear I cannot lift you." The musical voice reached my ears, and my heart swelled. She came, the Princess saved me; I held little doubt of her intentions. The fair and just woman, of this godless place meant to set me free. I had not realized in the depths of my despair, how much I wanted out of that dreadful prison.

"It is a horse, milady. His name is Achilles." I do not know why I chose now to reply to her earlier question. It seemed fitting since she alone released me. I sensed no other nearby, and felt her hands on my arm. Somehow, I would repay the kindness of this gentlewoman. Answering her curiosities of my world was a start. My world … how absurd that sounded.

"You must go now. I fear there is nowhere safe nearby, perhaps anywhere in the land. My people plan to kill you if you stay. You must head south, milord." She removed my covering. My vision returned fully, but I blinked and adjusted my eyes. The Princess stood before me in her glorious beauty. The three moons were high, but her face hidden from me. *Three moons*? My eyes widened and my jaw dropped. *I was in another world*.

"I am lost in this land without my armor, without my sword ..." Without any knowledge of beasts that stalked prey, human or whatever their race was. I did not want to admit that my fate remained the same. These lands, the creatures, I knew not what I faced out there in the bitter wilderness, or within the walls of this castle.

"I could not get either, but I stole what I could from the keep cache. In the pouch by your side are medicine, bandages, a map, and food too. There is enough for a few days." The Princess cut my binds, and handed me the jeweled dagger.

She turned to leave, but spun around. The Princess curtsied and added, "May my Gods watch over you."

"Come with me," the words left my lips. I could not explain why I asked. She was naught but a stranger and surely, she would slow me down. Perhaps the terror of this world drove me to ask her. Maybe it was because of all the women I had ever met, none affected me on this level. My heart beat at the mere thought of her. A good woman, and she would make ... I shook the thoughts from my mind.

"You must go. It is only a matter of time before your absence is noticed, my Lord, or mine. I fear I cannot go, even if I wanted to." Her tone softened me. The Princess did want to flee this place.

A bell ripped through the calm night. Within moments, I found us surrounded by elves. I knew I could still maneuver about the half sleeping and half drunk, by the smell of it, elven guard. Time ran short, however, we fled together now, or I left the Princess to the demise of her people. They would know without a doubt that she freed me, and that, I decided, I could not live with.

I leapt upon Achilles, and without asking again, I lofted the Princess up. She squealed but did not fight. Together we tore into the night with not a sound between us. She shed no tears for her capture, and she screamed no words. The Princess just sat there in front of me, still as stone. I did not dare to look behind us, though we were not pursued. My brow puzzled, scrunching as I pieced it together. None of it made any sense. If this Princess was the King's daughter, riders would have been fast on the captor's tail. They would show no mercy.

I clicked my tounge, and pressed Achilles hard and fast, until the sun arose on the horizon. I laughed when only one sun arose. The sky painted itself in hues I could not recall. I became lost in the beauty, until I felt the warmth of the princess lounge against my chest. I slowed my charger's pace to a trot, as we approached a pristine silver lake, surrounded in a blanket of white snow. It was serenity at its best.

~~~

"Princess," his silken, foreign voice whispering my title. My eyes blinked, burning from the sun. He awoke me from a splendid dream that quickly turned to a nightmare. I shivered and opened my eyes wide; we were still atop the magnificent beast. The human's, strong arms wrapped around me. No, I did not want him to let me go. His warmth was all I had left in this world.

Yet I knew it could never pass. That was all I ever agreed upon with mother. No man would ever want me for what I was. I would muster a passing curious glance, until the wrappings came off.

"My Lord, we have made quite a distance," the words left my tired mouth, and a yawn followed. The horse brought us to the small lake south of my kingdom. We were safe from the water nymphs until nightfall.

"Achilles must rest," his voice was short and it warmed my cheeks, with embarrassment. Oh, of course the beast would require rest after such a long distance. The man too as he had not slumbered to my knowledge.

"Do you have a plan, my Lord?" I asked, wondering if he knew how to return to Midgard. It was improbable that anyone save the Seelie Court would know how. They held the other gate to the Bifrost which connected the Nine Realms of the universe. Our court had them too, but I knew better than to trust any of them.

"Nay, I know nothing of your world. I wish only to return to mine." His voice held something I did not understand. Pain, anguish, and annoyance those I understood. This, however, was an emotion I did not know well, but it reminded me of grief. Had he left a great love behind in his world? My legs slid down from Achilles. Yes, grief that was what I decided. Love …

My shoulders fell forward. If mother bore witness to my behavior, she would have corrected me. That I would not miss, yet I knew marriage did not cease my punishments. My hands folded and unfolded, as I turned away. A Princess acted a certain way. No indiscretions allowed. There was no love in my future, and I craved my freedom. How could I love a man that held consorts? How could Drust love me if I could not give him all he needed: an heir.

"We should have a plan." I reached for a stick, but the branch refused to break. "It will take time to reach the Seelie Court, perhaps too long. I could always ask Prince Drust for help." The man said nothing in return. His silence churned my belly.

"I do not possess the power to send you home, milord-" The man slid down from his horse and my eyes followed the thick curve of his body. Knotted muscles flexed in his arms, bulkier than any elf or faerie. He stepped forward, his mouth curling beneath the dark whiskers. My race did not have such hair and I wanted to explore it.

"Please, Princess Morgana, call me Thomas." I blinked, as he walked closer. Too near for the informal setting, but we were outlaws now. We stood face to face with only inches apart. I found myself drawn to his heavy lidded gaze. His eyes were unlike any of my kind. Speckles of blue, grey, and green danced in them. They held wisdom, pain, and emotions I had never known another to suffer besides me.

"Thomas," I repeated slowly, and a grin spread across his face. The rough and gruff exterior melted, giving way to a fine man. I smiled beneath the veil, and he grasped my hand. Thomas brought it to his rough lips and kissed my knuckles. An ache spread in my chest, and I could not explain the sensation. My heart, the bumbles jumped from my stomach and into my heart.

Thomas winked. "Aye, milady, very good, and you are the Princess Morgana."

"It is only fair, Thomas that you call me Morgana, or Mori." I took sharp breaths trying to regain composure. "I am not your noble, and we are far from your home." He raised an eyebrow, and appeared deep in thought over my askance. His eyes raked over me, as if drinking me whole. For the first time I felt uneasy, my cheeks burning hot beneath the silk covering my face. Deep down I knew I was not the type of prize one sought. Damaged, burned, and easily discarded was the Princess Mori.

I strolled toward the water, but Thomas grasped my arm. Elves were quick, and I easily escaped his grip. I was sure he merely meant to thank me. There was no use in filling my head with silly notions of love or fairytales. One look at me, the real me, would send any gentleman running for the hills.

"Pri, err Morgana, what are you?" Thomas asked softly.

I laughed, and turned around. "I am an elf of the Unseelie Court."

"An elf …" His eyes fell away, and his brow wrinkled.

"Cousin to the Faerie and Dwarf, we are no relation to the draconic race; though they too reside here along with other creatures. They do tend to keep to themselves." With the exception of the dragons, all three races divided between the Seelie and Unseelie courts. The exact numbers were unknown. Both had elves, faeries, and dwarves. Although dwarves were cousins to the faeries, the only difference between an elf and a faerie were the wings. Dwarves were smaller, and witnessing a human now, they appeared closer in relation than to my kind.

"Of course." He glanced to me and smiled.

"Hard to wrap your mind around?" I knew it was difficult. Thomas spent his life not knowing of the realms, of magic, or even the many races. To be thrown into a world, captured, and come but mere hours from death …

"More than you could fathom," he muttered, but I heard his words. Anger and pain painted them, and I understood. More than he realized, I understood what it meant to live as an outsider. Even in my own world, I was an outcast, but I was alone no longer. A grin smoothed over his face, and I returned it.

Thomas would need me on his journey, and I would accompany him for as long as possible. Eventually, they would find me, I would depart, and return to the life destined to me. For now, I knew he needed me to stay. Perhaps, I did not want to leave.

~~~

"What do you mean she is gone? Have you sent no one after her?" I screamed at the Queen, the King, and their useless son. If anyone harmed my Princess, they would all suffer the wrath of the dragon, of all the dragons. My fists clenched, and I fought for control.

"Prince Drust, we have sentries out now," the Queen's voice was cold. She made it easy for others to know of the hatred. I on the other hand grew fond of Mori, though I knew I could never give her what she deserved. Morgana was an elf, and I was not. Our races did not mix. They could not breed dragons. For her I made an exception after witnessing the cruelty of the Queen.

If I were King, her fate would have proven much different. With massive armies in tow, I would march upon their lands until the Queen surrendered. I had no cause to harm anyone save her. Mori had confided all of her sins to me, and my blood boiled for revenge.

In the beginning, it was to scare me off, for as much as she wanted freedom, the Princess wanted someone to love her. Love her, I did. Dragons did not love, but somehow I did. My hands folded over my chest. How did Mori disappear?

"Which way did they leave? Was Morgana forced? Someone better tell me how this even happened." Veins pulsed in my face. Anger swept over me, and I knew bloodied rage would follow.

"She encountered a human, sire." I snorted, eyeing the guard I entrusted with her safety. Yet no one told me anything I did not already know. If Mori left on her own, I would ensure her safety, and leave her in peace even if that meant allowing the human to live. If this vile human stole her away, then there were no words to describe the torture I would personally inflict.

"We do not know how the prisoner escaped, or how our dear Mori …" I raised a hand to silence the elven witch. My head ached from her lies and deceit. I would not stand there while she pretended to give a shit about her daughter. Mori was the only female that proved strong enough to survive her.

After nineteen years of torture, the Queen still had the gall to call her weak. I did not know a single dragon who would have survived. For that strength, and her gentle kindness, I would see to her safety. It was why I fell in love with her … if only it was enough. I wished the Gods had made her a dragon, a proper mate, and I would shun my consorts for eternity. A smile formed on my lips at the thought of losing them all, well maybe not eternity.

Chapter Three
Hidden Pain

"**M**ori, can you help me?" I raised my head at my name rolling off his tongue. The accent tickled my ears pink. My thoughts wandered off, as I sat on the icy rock. Desperately, I was trying to recall a place to take shelter. Searching the map I took from the pack on the horse, I found one place. It was public, but without it, we could not expect to last the evening. The downfall was we were within the Unseelie lands, but it was a hair safer than open countryside.

"Yes, Thomas." I approached him but stopped to laugh. The man rummaged through the sack. He held up different packages I prepared for his journey. Food in his country must appear different.

"This." I held up a pouch filled with dried meat, fungus, and another contained nuts from Yggdrasil, the tree of life. The seeds were an elven cure all used when magic did not work. I kept it on hand for the times, which was almost always, that my Myst failed.

"Is the water safe here?" I did not understand what he asked. Thomas pointed to the lake, and made gestures to his mouth. I stifled another giggle, but my grin could not remain hidden. His features reddened with embarrassment.

"You wish to drink it? You would do better to collect snow. This lake is haunted." We did not need the wisps growing angry and leading us to our doom.

He sighed and grasped my hands. "Is there anywhere I can take you, anywhere you will be safe?"

My smile faded into a frown. I shook my head though, the dragon prince would never hurt me. If my family found me, well let them. The worst they could accomplish was death. I prayed to the Gods for it every night. Every morning I awoke to new tortures. Death, I welcomed it to take me to the Gates of Hel.

"We should depart soon. There is a town not far from here. I left money in the …" I pointed to the covering of the horse.

"Saddle." Thomas's voice was soft, and I ignored the concern etching upon his face.

"I left money in the saddle. There is an inn in the town nearby we can spend the night." Gold, silver and gems were our currency. As long as we had one of the three, we would have little problems. If not, many places took barter. All we had for barter was Achilles, and I would never ask Thomas to part with him. It became clear that he loved his horse. I did too.

"Will they not question Achilles? Your curiosity tells me you have no horses in this land." Yes, and hopefully it was enough of a distraction that no one realized Thomas was human. *There must be a bounty out by now on both our heads*, I thought. Those thoughts rummaged through my mind, but I stayed quiet.

"No, our beasts are similar, but they have wings. They are the Pegasus." I watched his eyes brighten. "You have heard of them?" He shook his head.

"There are stories, myths actually, that talk of the animals. In my world, we call them fairytales. They are often told to children." Children, one more grace I shall never know. That was for the best, perhaps. I would not risk turning into my mother.

"Do you tell them to your children, Thomas?"

"Nay, I do not have any children." He grinned. "I'm a bit young to settle down just yet." I let out a little laugh. He was not much older than I was.

"Our worlds are very different." I shook my head. "I should have already been married off. They are arranged here, for royal and the lower noble blood." My twin brother was next.

"It is not so different in my world. Few unions are ever because of love, and many do not believe in the notion at all." I nearly fainted. How could one not believe in love? Even though it was not for me, I still held faith in the notion, and I would until my dying breath.

I turned away, and my brows twisted. "That is a shame."

"Do you believe in it?" Thomas whispered, and I spun back. His long black lashes batted, as his lips curled into a smile.

"Love? Nay, not for me. I do believe it is possible, for others."

"Your gentleness and kindness toward me are cause for argument, Mori." I grew silent at his compliment. Only the Prince and my brother ever treated me as such. This would end the moment he saw me for what I truly was. That time drew closer with each passing second.

The town alone was a disastrous idea, unless I removed the wrappings. We were still close enough to my kingdom. Someone might recognize me. While the rumors spread of my ugly, disfigured face, no one outside of my family and Drust witnessed the destruction left by her Myst. I would blend in easier, as much as it pained me to show this side of myself to Thomas. The comfort I felt with him would fade; I would not blame him if he ran away in terror.

I wandered to the water. The dark surface lay frozen in some places. My legs lowered to the ground, and I knelt into the icy bank. I stared at my reflection. My mummified face stared back. Thomas paid no mind to my actions and remained by Achilles side, speaking gently to the beast.

With the silk across my face, only one of my eyes and lips remained visible. Thomas had not asked why yet, though I knew the time approached. Men always asked. Women chose to whisper and giggle behind my back. Mother held no sympathy for the imperfections her wrath brought me. Magic failed every time I attempted to heal the marks and scars.

I removed the hood of my blue traveling cape. Gently, I unraveled the smooth cloth covering my head. My heart raced, as it anticipated his reaction. I doubted he would shun me, but his warmth would

cool. There was no lying to myself. I enjoyed his attention and the way he looked upon me, even if it made
me nervous. Thomas was a man though, and they
enjoyed their pretty things. Pretty I was not.

Cold air rushed against my pale cavernous skin.
I blinked, allowing my bad eye time to adjust, as my
thoughts raced. Silence surrounded me except for
my heartbeat and breath. Puffed like silver in the air,
I centered myself upon it. I was naked; my unknown
face displayed for the realms folly. My head fell
toward the water. Looking at the reflection again, I
relived each moment. I bit back the tears filling my
eyes at the remembrances of each scar or bruise. The
deep gash across my eye flowed down into my cheek;
I was a child when her ice cut me. The mutilated ear,
I was a teen when mother burned it with her fire.
Some magically induced, but many physical wounds.
Healing and new marks littered my flesh on both
sides, but those would eventually heal. There were
wounds, however, that would never heal. Those cuts
and burns reached my soul and heart.

She turned something beautiful into a monster.
This fate I wished upon no one. My hands twisted
in my lap, clenching and unclenching at the thought
of my mother. Not a man, not a woman, and most
certainly not a child. No one should be made to
suffer at the hands of another. But I had borne each
mark and scar as a badge of courage and defiance.
Yet I could not find the strength now to face a com-
plete stranger. The disgrace of my life filled me to
the brim, and cascaded upon me like a raging water-
fall. I clutched my hands to my chest and cried. Not

because she hated me, but because I would never know anything else.

"Mori, are you alright?" he asked, but my lips quivered. Not words but sounds poured through the opening of my mouth. "Princess?"

~~~

I watched, as the Princess removed her coverings. It was an unusual custom for a woman of royal blood, but this was a new world. Who was I to question any of the oddities, which were most likely normal occurrences? Then she cried. No, that was an understatement. She wailed, clutching her breast.

Men in my world did not like when a woman shed tears. The notion and reaction bred into us. If a woman should cry, the man made it right. My lips pressed together, as she continued. That was the unspoken law of my kind.

I walked up to where she sat. My movements were slow and practiced, as to not startle her; I placed my hand upon her back. Mori stiffened under my touch. Gently I rubbed my hand upon the soft fabric of her cloak.

"Mori," I tried again, when it dawned on me that I might have been mistaken. At first, it seemed as if the Princess wanted to leave. Perhaps she grew homesick, or feared for her life. Maybe there was another waiting for her; with such a pure heart, any man would claim it. I would never harm her, or deliberately place her in its way, but she did not know this. Mori did not know the oath I took, when I became a Knight of the court. She did not know me.

"I do not know what came over me," her voice staggered, as Mori struggled. My heart broke for whatever pain she shouldered.

"There is no shame in crying, Mori. I will take you back to your home. You must miss your family." Even if it meant walking back into the den of lions, I would fix this. My heart disagreed, and the ache grew, piercing my insides.

"No, please you mustn't. I can never go back. Please, sir I beg of you." It was at that moment that I laid eyes upon the real Mori. The woman beneath the mask faced me, looking straight into my eyes, as she begged. Those violet eyes, cursed and scarred, pleaded with me. The anguish behind the mask grew in her silent contemplation.

"Mori, I ..." There were no words to describe the horrors left to her face. Deep scars, black, purple, and yellowed bruises cascaded down half of her visage. I could not see where they ended. Anger flooded my vision, as my nostrils flared. What type of monster did this?

Stunned into silence, and frozen with disbelief, I said nothing. Yet beneath it all, Mori remained the most beautiful creature I ever witnessed. The disfigurement told her past, yet her heart and soul were unlike any I encountered before. This woman risked much more than I realized, when she freed me, if this was what happened, before I came into her life.

I watched, as she bit her bottom lip and turned around. It tore at me in ways I did not understand. So she had scars ... I did too. Mori was not flawless; no one in this world or mine could claim perfection.

I found myself wanting something I could never have; I had no business wanting a Princess. In the end, I was no more than a measly, hated, outlawed Knight. It changed nothing. I was falling in love with her. From the first moment in the courtyard, I knew. She deserved better than me.

Before I knew what I was doing, I shifted to the side, and tilted her chin to force her gaze. Her eyes were the color of lavender. I ran a thumb gently along the scar below the left eye, and found myself wondering how it happened. Mori blinked, those flowery eyes still pleading silently with me. There was no way in hell, not even for the promise of my home, would I ever send her back.

I pulled the Princess closer to me. Enveloping her with my arms, I felt the frailty of her in that moment, as her chest shuddered against mine. My heart throbbed a little bit faster, when she was near, but I ignored it. I ran my fingers against the mass of midnight hair, tangled and braided as it might be, comforting her, I told myself.

Shame rose in my throat, as I used her weakness as an excuse to feel her warmth in my hands again. Marks passed us by, as the sun set, and I held her, vowing silently to never let harm come to Mori ever again. Yes, there was no other answer aside from love.

Whispering into her ear, as to not spoil the moment, I asked her, "Mori, you know I must ask. Who in your household harmed you?" I could not envision it being the Prince. Sure, I had but a few moments in his presence, but it was enough. He cradled Mori to his body, carrying her little form as if guarding her.

"It is not so simple, Thomas." She sniffled. "There is much about my world that you do not know. Just as there is plenty in your world, which would seem strange to me."

"Aye, but we do not harm women." I allowed my bitterness to spill into my words. Knights followed a code of conduct that revolved around chivalry and honor. While in the heat of battle some men committed unspeakable offenses, nobles were left untouched upon penalty of death. That was why I could not understand the abuse. The bruises were new, terribly fresh; it was not an old crime.

She untangled herself from my embrace. I shivered and stood as Morgana did. Every step I took, she took another away from me. Times such as this, I wished I had paid Sir Percival more attention, when he spoke of his conquests with women. No woman caught my eye before Mori. Sure, there were plenty of lovely ladies to gaze upon, but they were cold and self-serving. What was I to do? I let my breath release in a hiss. Did I chase after her? No, I thought, as she walked away. Mori deserved a proper courting and nothing else would do.

"On an everyday level, I would agree," she said. "It is not common amongst anyone here. Sometimes it happens … I had to show you." Mori faced me. "Now I seek no pity, but my people know my covered likeness, and we are still within the Kingdom of the Elves of the Light." A slight sound left her lips, but I could not tell its meaning. Mori stopped speaking, but I motioned her to continue, as I prepared Achilles for departure.

"It will take us two days to cross into the realm of the Dragon. I hope my dear friend Prince Drust will offer you freedom in return for my safety."

My mouth fell open. She used those words before. To say it frightened me was no lie. Yet she did not appear scared at all, perhaps because she grew up in this realm. My eyes darted toward the sky, but there were no beasts. Maybe Mori held an admiration for this Prince of Dragons, or she felt something deeper.

"Do you love him?" Jealousy arose in me at the thought of her loving anyone other than me. It made no sense, as Mori deserved it more than anyone else did. Besides, I may be a believer of love, but it was something that was much akin to a flower. You plant the seed of love, and patiently it bloomed into a deep unmoving affection.

Her hands twisted, and she cocked her head. "I told you before, love is not in my future … as a friend, yes I do have love for him, but I am not in love with him." Relief washed over my whole body. There was nothing worse than finally falling in love and then finding out her heart belonged to another. Nevertheless, she was wrong. Adoration and affection were in her future, as long as I remained.

I was uncertain if I could even return to my home. After all, I trotted right into this one. If it were that easy, why had the guards not turned me around, and sent me back? No, even if I could go back to England, to Earth, I did not think I could leave Mori behind to the dragons.

"Is he really a dragon?" Her laughter filled the air, and I smiled at the mere sounds. After what she just went through it was just what the physician ordered, yet it did nothing to settle my nerves. The idea of a gigantic winged beast, being anything but fearful, did not match the mythology of my world. It was often said they once inhabited my realm, but that was long before my time.

She smiled. "Yes, when he wants to be. I think he would like you very much."

"Why is that?" I cocked my head out of curiosity.

"You do not judge me like the others do, Thomas." Her hand fell to my shoulder, as I packed the map away. "Mother makes me hide, father ignores me, and my brother rescues me, yet never stops it, until it has begun. The servants whisper, the women laugh, and until you only the Prince treated me like the marks did not exist." I turned and took her hands in mine. They were smooth and warm, but not unused like the royalty back home. Looking deep in her eyes, I found amusement and laughter, where there was pain naught moments before. I knew then and there, that I was within my right to take her from the castle. My code as a Knight demanded it.

"Princess Mori, I promise you this. I will allow no one to lay their hands upon you ever again." I meant it, every single word. Achilles snorted in agreement.

"That is a sweet sentiment, Thomas. I appreciate the vow, but the damage is not from hands but from magic." I mouthed the word: magic. Magic, how could this be? I shook my head. Such things simply did not exist.

"Magic? We do not have magic in my world. In fact, it is blasphemy. We call it witchcraft." It was a sin to practice the art of witchcraft. In my world, they burned witches and warlocks.

"Magic is very real, Thomas. The Faerie King gifted it to all the realms. We are not witches; we do not use ritual to conduct magic. The proper way is to ask of the elements, to pray to the Gods, and if they see fit then your wish is granted."

My hands tightened around hers, but mindful not to hurt her. I wanted to know something, but I did not understand how to ask. What God or element had agreed to harm her? It felt hateful, spiteful even, if someone like Mori could fall to harm.

"Worlds and Gods ... there is more than this one and my own?" I asked in amazement. There were other religions besides Christianity on Earth. They taught us to believe in a one true God. Mori nodded her head and pressed her lips together. She shifted her eyes and took a sharp breath. Did she not wish to tell me?

"Sadly, you landed closest to the Unseelie Court. Apart from me, no other in this Kingdom likes humans. This is why we must reach the dragons. Their position is neutral, and perhaps they may grant passage to the southern realm of the Seelie Faeries." I shook my head in disbelief. I was more than just another outsider. This world may not accept Mori with her imperfections, but at least they did not hunt her because of them. To risk the wrath of a dragon ... I was unsure what was actually more dangerous: the road or a leviathan beast that may or may not like me.

"Wait, but you are an elf? How are you involved with the faeries?" I became beyond confused the more Mori told me. All her words jumbled together and I scratched my head. Every time she answered one of my questions, there were three new ones to ask. How many had I already asked? This world fascinated me, it truly did, yet deep down I knew I would either die here, or watch Morgana marry a man she did not love. Nevertheless, would she ever love anyone, or truly allow herself the chance to fall in love with a mere human like me?

"Elves are a member of the Faerie race. So are pixies, brownies, gnomes, dwarves, and so on. Faerie is just a general term." If I lived through this day, nay this adventure, I would have one heck of a story to tell, when I returned home. If I ever went home again, I refused to leave this world empty handed. Would she forgive me if I stole her away for good?

~~~

I could not wait around a moment longer. It became clear that neither the Queen nor King of Alfheim cared about Mori's well-being. The only one who shared my concern was her brother. Yet he did nothing to defy the family.

The Prince of Alfheim was a coward in my eyes. While I did not expect him to save the human, I could not fathom leaving Mori. Surely the creature had kidnapped her. I refused to entertain the facts suggesting she released him. That was the argument her guard presented me, the guard I gave to her. The captain failed to protect her, and I would most certainly deal with him in the near future. Morgana remained my top priority.

It fell to my kind. The dragons would hunt down this human. The thought left a dirty taste in my mouth. The magic protecting this realm barred entry of outsiders. This was especially true for those on Earth. Now not only had it failed, but this man stole my sweet, innocent Mori too.

Images flashed through my mind as I rode out. The human's lips kissing her flesh threatened the bile to rise. Mori must be frightened out of her wits.

~~~

Morgana this, Morgana that … Morgana never should have survived in the first place. I let out an unbecoming sigh. As Queen, it fell on me to produce suitable, strong heirs to the throne. The girl was neither. Just a weak creature the Gods felt free to punish. Unlike her sisters, she lived to adulthood, and then to the proper age to marry.

"I have to find her," I spoke to myself. The plan ruined everything unless she returned. We needed the alliance, or the kingdom would fall, when the people realized the money was gone. The Dragon Prince offered a hefty sum to marry Morgana. It was more than we made the past fifty years.

My fists clenched at my lack of foresight. The kingdom was doomed unless she returned and married the dragon. How could Morgana do this to us? Did she wish ill of her family for trying to make her a stronger elf? Nay, she was still the spoiled bitch.

All her life I worked, I pushed her to use her gifts. Morgana was just too weak, not like her brother who remained strong in the art of magic and warfare. Now he would make a grand King one day ; I planned to change history, and pass my crown to a male heir. but Morgana was next in line unless she married the dragon. Even then she could claim the throne right from under our noses if the people supported her.

Yet the King blamed me just as much. I never took into account the possibility of a human entering the lands. Never did I expect Mori to release the vile human either. She brought shame to her family. The thought of what my daughter did sickened me, and her father was beyond furious. If she dared to return home, I knew what I had to do now. When the child returned, Mori would never again see the light of day. Morgana bore the greatest threat to our livelihood.

Chapter Four
Longawagon

Coming into Longawagon seemed like a fantasy. Little cottages lined the dirt road. Children of all sizes ran about the yards. Farther down, a full market place sat at its heart. Different but curious all the same. In my world, towns like this one did not exist outside of the immediate kingdom. If they did, they were a rarity.

In my realm, farmers grew crops and traded with one another. Very few families held wealth, and even nobility grew enough food for its household. Lords controlled the peasants, the Dukes or Earls in charge of the Lords, and all paid homage to the royal family. I saw none of that here. These creatures appeared as equals in my eyes.

"The inn is right up there," the Princess spoke in a hushed tone, her weight pressed against me, and arms wrapped about my waist. I almost did not hear her above the hustle and bustle of the people on the street, combined with my own deep thoughts.

"What should I do with Achilles?" The towns-folk were staring at my poor horse. I did not fear anyone harming him, but I imagined these people were curious. They were busy murmuring about him; no one seemed to even notice I was not a man of this realm too.

"It is best to stable him at the livery. With enough gold I can buy silence," she said, as she dismounted; I followed suit. To say I was not impressed was a lie. Mori was quite a capable woman all on her own. She knew how this world worked far more than I did. I would have to relent and allow her to do the talking from here on out. Even my accent seemed foreign.

"Do we have enough? I fear the only items of value I had were my armor and sword," I whispered. The armor was not anything special. The sword however, was a gift from the King of England. The blade swung true, but the jewels incrusted into the hilt could feed a family for years. It was irreplaceable, and meant as much to me as all the lands that he granted with it.

"We will need more, but I think we will be suf-ficient for a few more days. There is the livery up ahead. We'll walk to the inn after we tuck in Achil-les for the night." I watched, as she gave him a pat. Achilles seemed to eat up the attention, and paid no mind to the gawkers. My lips pressed in a grim smile. Silly horse, it must be nice to ignore the troubles facing the three of us.

A great uneasiness washed over me and glanced around for the source. There was not much out of the ordinary, but I pulled my cloak closer around my face.

I led my charger inside by his reigns. Mori spoke quickly with the fellow in a language I did not understand. His eyes widened at the mention of extra compensation, or I assumed as much when Mori rattled her coin purse. It seemed no matter where a person traveled, coinage always mattered above all else.

England and the world I came from were not any different. Everything came down to who had more land, gold, finer clothes, and silly notions. Growing up, and being one of many sons born to an Earl made me just as susceptible to that style of life. Yet when I vowed to train as a Knight, I left it all behind me. Instead, I preferred a far simpler life even if it was not what I found in the end. There was nothing simple in this realm or the outlaw life.

"The man will keep him until one of us comes for him. I promised more upon our leaving, as long as he keeps him safe, and tells no one of his presence. He'll have his work cut out for him seeing as fifteen or more watched us come in." I gave her a nod. We strolled toward the inn, when Mori abruptly stopped in the middle of the stone lined street. She spun around and stepped closer. My cheeks burned beneath the hood, and I was thankful for the setting sun.

"Thomas, I should ask you now. Would it be a great trouble if we must share quarters? The rooms are small, but if we pretend to travel as a pair there will be less suspicion, and if trouble does arise we can escape easier," Mori spoke rapidly, more so as if she were nervous. I watched her hands fidget and move as she talked.

"If you are uncomfortable we can make another arrangement. It is less money if we share is all," she added when I did not respond.

My head dipped into a bow. "Mori, milady, I am an honorable man, a Knight in my world. There are strict codes and oaths that I must uphold. Your reputation and honor are all that concern me. But you have my word, as a gentleman, to respect your wishes." Digesting her words, I saw one problem with the plan. There was no way I would share her room, let alone her bed, if it caused pain, trouble, or rumor.

She blinked, as a smile spread over her pink lips. "My honor is long broken, Thomas …" Mori laughed. "I am not married because of … the Prince wishes to marry me only out of some misguided notion."

I eyed her, as the words flew out of her mouth. Again, she grew uneasy and glanced away. Was it the marriage that worried her so? Why would she bother at all if she did not love him? Perhaps it was simply as any other royal marriage would be in my world. Mori hinted to it as being such.

"His family consented only as a part of a treaty. Drust means well, but if there is a way to leave the bargain and retain freedom, I would pounce on the chance." She snapped her fingers together. The excitement in her eyes had an empowering effect. When she spoke of freedom, Mori meant it, and I saw the drive in her violet eyes. It made her even more stunning, and my heart beat faster.

"Is that not what we're doing now?" I said with a smile and a wink, attempting to calm her down. Reaching for her hand, it surprised me when she did not pull away. Instead, she interlaced her fingers with my own, and beamed me a sweet smile, causing my heart to miss a beat.

"Aye, so let's get on with the façade. I am tired and a wee bit hungry. Just keep that hood up, until we are behind closed doors. If anyone asks say you're ill." I turned my head from her, feeling the frown wash down my face. Of course, how could I be so imprudent? This ... meant nothing ... was nothing ... my love meant nothing to Mori. A curse slipped out from under my breath. I was thankful she did not question it, and quickly changed the subject.

"I thought elves were immortal," I whispered, still looking away and trying to memorize the lay of the surrounding buildings in case we needed to escape.

"Thomas, not all that walk this world are what they appear. Some illnesses can claim us, and we are not immune to infection. Besides, the proprietor might be a gnome or a leprechaun." I turned to face her in what must have been shock. I watched the grin widen, and though I was not certain, I swore Mori gave me a wink. My heartache only grew.

"Thank you, Mori." I gave her hand a squeeze, trying to gauge her reaction.

"For what, Thomas?" she whispered back, but Mori returned the gesture. It gave me hope that perhaps she at the very least liked me. That was all I could hope for though, I wished for far more. I wanted to save her, as much as I wanted her to love me too.

"Everything. We shall earn your freedom even if I must die trying." I gave her hand another squeeze, and pulled her closer to me. In that moment

I realized, I never wanted to let her go out of my life, never out of my sight.

I wanted to be the one to prove her wrong about love. Without her friendship, I would not have witnessed another sunrise or sunset. I could start with friends. If she stayed, who knows how much different her fate would have fared.

"Excuse me, madam and sir, but what was that wonderful creature you rode in on?" An odd-looking man asked. If I had to guess … he looked like an elf, but he was far taller than the ones akin to Mori. His build was more akin to a gladiator, and his eyes appeared cat like.

"It is called a horse. They are quite rare sir," Morgana replied to the stranger, who looked at her questioningly, but she pulled us along the street before he could reply. A glance over my shoulder showed the man nodding to himself and scratching his head. Yes, these elves were the curious sort. I looked again, and the man's eyes glowed golden.

"That was not an elf was it, Mori?" I had to know what the creature was. In fact, I should have been doing more of that, and asking her questions about the world. If this was my home than these would all be things, I had to learn.

"That, Thomas is a Dragon disguised as an elf. You can tell from their height and eyes. Most elves are close to seven foot lengths tall, but dragons are even bigger." Lovely, I thought, now I would have to fight a foe larger than myself atop of Achilles. That was not my idea of a fair fight at all, because if this Prince stole Mori from me, I would fight to the death.

"Don't be alarmed, milord. They really are a neutral sort. It was a part of their treaty when they crossed over."

"What do you mean?" I asked her, stopping her before the door. She seemed annoyed, but I did not want to forget to ask.

"Thomas ..." She sighed and peered around me. "Only the faeries and elves are the original inhabitants of this realm. Over the centuries, others moved in from the other eight realms. The dragons were the last before the Faerie King barred the portals. They come from the Niflheim, the Realm of Myst. Many fled the evil queen who was known for taking the lesser races as slaves, therefore they were ordered to remain neutral for as long as they made this their home," Mori whispered, drumming her foot, and I tried to keep up with all she said.

"Has there ever been a ... one of ... you know." I did not want to say human.

"You're the first that I know of, but it is possible I am wrong. Elves live a long time, but I have only been around for nineteen winters. Now can we please get inside before someone notices you're ... you?" Her tone filled with more frustration, but her face told me otherwise. I think she liked my questioning in general, but perhaps asking them in the middle of town was not the greatest idea.

"After you, milady." I smirked, opening the heavy door for the most beautiful princess in all the lands. Now we needed to make it through the night, and I must find a way to talk her out of this dragon alliance nonsense. He remained a last resort. We would find another way.

~~~

The brick inn shocked me. My pulse quaked, as I spoke with innkeeper. He tended the bar too. There were no questions or ill behavior either. Thomas remained hidden beneath his cloak, wrapping it about himself. The innkeeper said nothing to me about my hooded companion, nor did he bat an eye at our need for a room. A single room at that and if I knew how easy it was, I would have made this our first stop.

Regardless, the inn gave hope for Thomas and I to rest. He could not sleep while we rode, as I had before. Some elves conjured lodgings, but my magic could not. Aside from the inn, there was another option, and that entailed sleeping with Achilles. Not to be all princessy, but given the choice between sleeping with animals or the inn, well I chose the lodgings. This gave us the ability to recuperate for a few days, but after that, we must move on. Thomas suggested we depart on the morrow, but I was not accustomed to travel.

"We should sleep in shifts," I said, not wishing to speak of earlier in the road, and he gave a nod. For a man he did not speak much. Though he did ask many questions, it was not endless babble and rambling for the sake of his own voice. Men in my realm enjoyed hearing themselves speak. In other ways, it was nice. I could actually think up a plan that would benefit us both. Rather one that did not include the gallows, but freedom instead.

Why my people would execute such a handsome man went beyond my comprehension. In and out, Thomas was a decent man, and he cared. I hid my smile; he cared for the likes of me. Foolish notions would not serve either of us.

This was the same thought that played through my head every time our eyes met, or our hands touched. Part of me considered telling him, but it changed nothing. At the end of the day, he remained an outlaw. Even the Seelie Court would view him as such, but they would not execute a human. I held faith that my kin to the south would send Thomas home. Besides, I doubted he felt anything real toward me. Thomas' reactions were because I saved his life. If he felt anything, it was misguided. Even as I studied my reflection in the basin of water, I knew the truth. My heart, battered and beaten, could not survive. The fantasy of an us, was just that.

Before stabling Achilles, I removed the sack containing our food. Once in the quaint room, I pulled it from my cloak pocket. Our small room had one table, two chairs, and a small bed. Near the table lay a round window, blocked by Thomas' broad shoulders. His cloak hung from the bedpost, and it was the first time I saw him in the light without it.

I placed the stale bread and two strips of dried meat on the table. The rest I left in the pouch, secured within my cloak. I sat, the chair squeaking, as I pulled it out. He joined me, and we ate our meal in silence. Truthfully, I would rather have purchased a ladle of stew, but money did not allow for frivolous spendetures. As of right now, there were plenty of rations until I could figure the currency out. I did have more items of value, but I did not want to cash them in quite yet.

Thomas stretched his limbs, and removed his boots. I was hyperaware of every movement he made, every breath he took. It left a thickness in the air between us that grew with each moment, and it would not end until he slept.

Shifting in my seat, I withdrew my spyglass to clean the lens with a scrap of cloth. I busied myself; I needed a distraction from his seascape eyes, which bore into me even now. Why did he make this difficult, and was he not afraid for his own heart? Human and elf, the notion was laughable.

My breath released, and I sucked it in again. I arose and strolled to the window. There was nothing in particular I sought out, but the silence between us brewed further. I had to be strong for the both of us. Something told me to not let my guard down with him. Code or not, if I allowed anything to bloom, it would be the death of us both. Shaking my head, I tried to think back to a plan.

If Drust were as honorable as Thomas was then he would protect us. Maybe he could offer safe passage for Thomas to my cousin's lands. Then he could go home, and I would let myself settle down with Drust. If Thomas remained safe, if my Knight could go home.

My eyes welled with tears at the mere thought. Damn it, perhaps it was too late for my heart, but it was not for Thomas. No, I would see that he returned from whence he came. I was positive with his charm and good looks that women fell at his feet. He made a dashing prize, and someday he would have his pick of brides. Never again would he think of me, and that was for the best.

His soft footsteps fell behind me, and the bed gave a slight creak. Thomas laid himself upon the bed, and I thought he meant to sleep. Deciding it was safe to sit back at the little table, I took a candle that I purchased from the innkeeper, and lit the wick.

It was time to fashion a new pair of ears for Thomas, well I would at least try. In all reality, it might not work at all. Left alone to my own devices, I was crafty, but I never attempted to sculpt wax or ears. With his short hair, his ears stuck out. Our ears were not rounded; all the races, including the dwarves had pointed ears. If I could solve that problem then it would allow more freedoms.

"What are you doing over there?" he asked me, as I dripped a pool of wax onto the table. Thomas arose and the heat of his words grazed my neck. My palms dampened and my heart raced. His hand rested upon my shoulder. I held my breath without even realizing it. The room spun under his touch, and the bumbles assaulted my stomach.

"Trying to make you a set of ears," I mumbled after allowing my breath to release in a smooth exhale. Thomas turned me to face him, his fingers hooking my chin. My heart demanded it be let out of my chest. It pumped hard enough to make me dizzy. I told myself. Thomas was judging the destruction upon my face again. I willed my heart to slow; I willed it to forget.

"One day, I will repay your kindness, Mori." My cheeks flushed under the gaze of his multi-colored eyes, and I looked away, turning myself back to the task. The coldness crept up, as he lay back upon the creaking bed. Relief washed over me, and I was thank-ful I had not done anything foolish. In truth, it took every ounce of strength not to kiss him.

Thomas said nothing more that evening. My inner voice was correct. His touches and tone meant nothing more than friendship. It was all for the best. I was an elf, and he was a human. Thomas was a Knight, and I was a Princess. His Knighthood meant nothing in this world. Though it made me wonder what it meant in his. In his world, did Knights and Princesses fall in love? I doubted it.

By the sounds of his snores, he slept deeply into the night. I worked on his new ears, until I felt they were perfect. At least as perfect as I could make them. When he awoke, I would fasten them on, and pray they worked. The more like an elf he looked, the better chance we had making it to the lands of the dragon.

~~~

Try as I might, I could not figure Mori out. They always said back home that it was an impossible task to understand a woman. Until now, I never believed any of the men that spouted it off, as if it were gospel.

The simple truth I wanted to know was, her ,beyond the scarred beauty. Beneath the bruises lay a woman of great wisdom and an honest charm. Her eyes reminded me of wild flowers, when she became excited. I was foolish enough to know, I loved her.

I found myself wanting to make her smile, but I did not know how. Every time I opened my mouth, she took pity or embarrassment from my words. How could I prove that I wanted her company, because she truly was a wonderful, intriguing woman?

Each moment with her, I decided to cherish. Her presence was a blessing. I just wish I knew how she felt about me. Could she ever love me, a simple human with nothing to offer her but my heart? My hands remained forever empty in this world. Like her, I had no magic, just years of training as a warrior. Was it enough for her?

If I were an elf, born to this land with magic, the answer would remain simple. Nevertheless, I was human and not a part of this world. A constant reminder with every breath I took. I was living because of her, and now we both lived, on borrowed time.

Morgana did more than anyone for me. Even back home, my brothers by blood and the brother-hood, would not go this far. Why did she do it for me if she did not care for me? Should I take it as a sign of hope? I did not know the answers I sought. All I knew was what my beating heart told me, what my mind said was truth. It screamed for me to not give up hope for her love.

I realized, as I let my heart rest, I wanted to stay. There was no world for me without Morgana. If I could not have her love then I did not wish to breathe. We must avoid the Dragon Prince's lands. I had yet to begin showing her the love and devotion I offered. My heart pounded at the thought, and I would show her, yes. Prove to her that she was capable and deserving of true love.

Eventually the thoughts ceased, as the war between what was right and wrong settled. My plan formed, the first moment after I awaken; I vowed to show Mori how much I loved her. I would show her, whether she liked it or not. That was my fate. There were no accidents. I was brought to this world for a reason. She had to believe me …

"You love what you should not," a voice spoke in the darkness. The accent thickened, and I struggled to understand his odd words. He almost sounded like the raiders of the North from Earth. I was dreaming, but it felt very real.

"Who is there?" I asked, wondering who haunted my dreams.

"My name is not important." A torch lit the darkness. Before me stood an old man. He wore no adornments, and reminded me of a monk or a priest. The oddest part of him was the eye patch covering his left eye; a scar pokes out from the top and bottom. It reminded me of Mori immediately. His hair though, was a reddish blond.

"Why shouldn't I love Morgana?" I assumed this dream was my brain and heart trying to connect, or ease my worries.

"To begin with, you should never have met her, but if you want more reasons I'm sure I can come up with more." His words and accusing tone unsettled me.

My teeth grit and ground.

"I didn't ask to cross into this world, but I would do it again if I had to." To think … Morgana still in the hands of those who wished to harm her. My head shook on its own. "I would do it again and again. I love her, I want to protect her."

"How are you certain it isn't gratitude or your honor that makes you think you love her?"

I blinked. "Old man, you will watch your tone."

The man walked a fine line and my veins throbbed in my skull. I would not allow him to raise any doubt. I thought it all through. It made sense, his words, but this was different. Mori and everything she encompassed was different.

"Tell me how you know, Sir Thomas," his voice was softer, and his glowing blue eyes took the appearance of compassion.

"It's hard to explain … when she speaks, I hear music. When I touch her hand, I get odd sensations here." I pointed to my stomach. "When I look at her, or breathe in her scent, my heart races. I did not want to leave her side … It sounded foolish. We just met, but I know. I just know, that to be without her would be asking me to stop breathing." the tears rolled down my face, as if they were real. My knees hit the ground that I could not see before. Like a broken man, I bowed at the man's feet. "I love her as I've never loved another."

"Will you uphold your oath, your code as a Knight?" Why was he asking me of this? What did it have to do with? Of course, I would. "Thomas, will you?" The man asked again, and I nodded. "Yes."

"Do you promise to hold faith in your heart and spread it for the good of your fellow man?"

"Yes." I glanced up to the man, noticing he was far taller than I. He was taller than the elves and dragons too. "I promise even without Mori, I would promise this to you."

Forever and until my last breath, I remained a Knight. The code and honor of my station, I always upheld those notions of sacrifice and safety. Without my kind, spreading our faith and goodness, many fell to evil bastards of the world. Was this realm any different?

Yellow-white light erupted from his hands. My eyes widened, and I sought away from him. The man who appeared feeble held me down, as the light bathed over my body. It entered my mouth, and the energy rolled down my throat. I choked.

"Rise, Sir Thomas Graftfield, the First Paladin and, Protector of Alfheim. May the light protect you and the weak. May you heal the sick, and defend those who deserve the protection of the Light. You have proven yourself worthy." My head swam, as he spoke. What did he mean? What did this change? Who was this man?

"Who are you?" I asked, cocking my head. My hands trembled "What have you done to me?"

"Who I am is of no importance. I gave you a gift to help you on your quest. You will need it." The older man snapped his fingers, and I was back in the room with Morgana.

Chapter Five
The Best Laid Plans

At the time, arriving home to regroup seemed like an excellent plan. However, nothing anyone told me made sense. The Dragon Council said not to worry, and that Princess Morgana would return. When I confronted them about the human, they became irritated.

"Your Grace, her parents claim they have the matter under control. Your parents are neither worried nor concerned." I hissed in return. Future bride or not, Mori was my friend.

"Perhaps, this is the Princess telling you she is not interested. Maybe it is best to call off ... well there isn't anything to call off yet." My temper faltered, and I walked away. I would not hear the end of it, if I ate one of the council for supper. He did have a point, but I wanted to hear it from Mori's lips.

"Sire," my personal weasel of a butler bowed, and I motioned for him to continue. "News just arrived about a strange creature being held at a livery in Longawagon. A strange woman, who was described as scarred, paid to board a black creature." As soon as the word scarred left Geoffrey's lips, I headed for the door.

"Your Grace, they said she is also with another, a male. She claimed they were together, and they are staying at the inn." My steps halted. Struggling to remain in control of my façade, I felt the battle turn against me. The arched entryway loomed ahead, and I ran full force, barely making it through. Before I knew it, I transformed into my natural state. Shimmering in the sunlight, my green wings buffeted, and I arose high into the sky, leaving a streak of green in my wake.

"Mori, I come to ssave you. My dear ssweet Mori, I sshall kill the human," I hissed, as I sped away on my journey to Longawagon.

~~~

If Thomas did not wake soon, I swore under my breath, I would dump water over his head. Right as I readied myself to pour, he shot up in a daze. After a moment, his eyes fell to me, and I read the disappointment behind them.

"It's about time you awoke. Here I thought you would sleep clear until sundown. Humans must need an awful amount of rest. You have been out for over twelve ticks. I am out of my mind with exhaustion ..." I stopped when I realizing I babbled like a child, and I turned away from him. The way he looked at my face, it hurt my belly. It was as if I awaited something more, ridicule or a jib, but Thomas said nothing.

"I'm sorry, Mori. Humans tend to sleep for many hours. Elves I take it, do not." I shook my head, and walked to the window. The sun would set in just a few hours. Pulling my glass from my pocket, I gazed aimlessly out of the window. Thomas rose up, and his soft footsteps came close to where I stood. The heat of his body warmed me.

"Mori, um … I had this odd dream. Bizarre is more like it." His voice sounded odd, rough and filled with confusion. I said nothing, for what could I say in response to this incomprehensible prattle. Instead, I put the spyglass down on the sill of the window, and stepped away. Thomas picked it up, and brought it back to me. The metal rolled in his hands, and he stared at it.

"Thomas, come sit down, and let me try these on. You can tell me as I work, and then I will check on Achilles while you eat." He nodded, and I turned to relight the candle. It was all I had to adhere the wax, but first I made sure the skin was clean.

"There was a man I had never laid eyes on before. He was old, but strong and able in the dream. He wore a patch over his eye." It sounded like Odin or Freyr paid him a visit. They were the most powerful of the Gods, though they rarely went to humans in their dreams. In fact, neither would go to a human male unless he was his son. Was Thomas a demi-god?

I filled the basin with water from the pitcher that I almost dumped on his head. With a swab of cloth, I dipped it in, and then swabbed it against his skin. There was a hum of Myst radiating from him. It was not there before he slumbered, but I kept silent, as he retold the tale of his dream.

"Thomas, did the old man have a staff or perhaps large birds with him?" Odin had two ravens, Huginn and Muninn. They represented thought and memory and aided the God. He also carried a staff and was missing an eye.

"He had no animal, but he held a torch, and a sword. The man held magic, Morgana. It was …" His eyes were wide as he spoke. The Myst did that. I smiled at the few memories I had. Invigorating, yes I knew what it felt like during my small surges of power.

"I believe you had a visitor. That is good news. It means we have the Gods on our side." I felt the smile widen on my face.

"I only believe in one God, Mori.' He shook his head, and I grasped it in my hands. "If that is who visited me, I do not know. I fear … I fear what he has given to me. I do not wish to harm …" he shook his head again, and I sighed. Placing both hands on his shoulders, he stilled with my touch. Thomas should not fear what the Gods chose to gift him, yet I understood. Magic was not present in his race. To humans, as he said, it was a crime.

"We will worry about it later. Let me get these set. I really am tired, Thomas." My voice was small, and I fought to keep my eyes open. I still had Achilles to check on too. In response, he reached for my hand. It startled me, when he brought it to his lips, and kissed my palm. Shivers rushed over my skin and into my cheeks.

"Sorry," he mumbled, and I peered at the back of his head. What was that for?

I resumed cleaning the ear, again. Once the lobe appeared unsoiled, I dripped wax along the top of the lobe. Thomas winced, but I soothed him the best I could. With my free hand, I cupped his face from behind, and rubbed my thumb over the sharp growth of his beard to relax him. When enough wax dripped, I quickly fastened the ear. I did not know if it was sheer luck or magic, but it held true.

"How does it look?" Thomas asked in a rough voice that I did not expect. I blinked, and moved in front of him to make sure the ears sat equally. I was not prepared to meet his half-lidded stare, or the way it drank me in wholly. When Thomas gazed upon me in that way, it made it impossible to breathe or move. I was like a fauna frozen with fear, except I was not afraid of him.

"It is passable, but how does it feel?" I hoped I had not pained him too much. Where the wax met the skin, it appeared reddened.

"A bit tender, but I will live." I nodded, and busied myself with anything that did not involve looking at Thomas. Once done with my task of cleaning up, I prepared to see Achilles. Thomas grabbed my hand, as I tried to walk away.

"Mori, do you ... I ... If we ... I" His eyes searched the room. The action was bizarre, and unexplainable. Was he was scared? Whatever it was, he needed to say proved difficult to articulate the words. Was he trying to tell me what I already knew? Did he realize how he looked at me? I could save him the pain of the words. It was the least I could do, for him.

"There is no need, Thomas," I said colder than I wanted and walked out of the room. I was not gone for more than a breath, when the door swung open, and Thomas grabbed my arm. He pulled me back into the room, the fear still set into his features.

I smoothed the creases from my dress. My eyes bore into him and my jaw twitched. What was his problem? I was no mind reader, but still he did not speak his mind. My eyes fell to his hand on my arm, and he followed my gaze.

"What do you want, Thomas?" He parted his lips, but no sound came out. I sighed and tugged myself from his grip. A flash of green caught my eye from the window. There was a dragon in the sky, I was sure of it. I turned myself away from him, and walked back to the window. My eyes slanted; elves and faeries held excellent sight. Thomas handed me the spyglass from the table. Spyglass in hand, I peered out again into the violet sky.

"Dragons," I allowed the whisper to roll off my tongue. Thomas, followed me to the window, and yanked the glass from my hand. My brow rose, and I spun around, but he held my glass to his eye.

"I don't see anything, Mori." His breath danced past my ear. The feelings returned to my stomach; I felt as if I were falling. Falling in love … with a human.

"I can see over ten miles out in detail without the spyglass, Thomas. We must depart soon. The townspeople are at risk. It will be better if they find us outside of the village." Did they come just for me, or did they hunt Thomas?

"No, if we run, we run. If you want to go with the Prince, so be it. I can't stop you." Anger, and something else I did not understand, rolled off him. I stood there stunned and hurt, as he sauntered out the door. I wanted to ask what he meant. I told him before there was no want. It was either go home, or with Drust. I would not return home.

With him gone, the room grew cold. Tears filled my eyes. I did not know what to do. If only someone had prepared me for this. I knew nothing of this, nothing of these feelings except that my heart broke no matter what road I chose. But if I stayed with Thomas, I could hold on to the love and respect for just a little longer. My heart pumped harder and the bumbles maddened with joy. I grabbed my belongings, and ran for the livery. Thomas would not leave, not without Achilles.

~~~

Without another word, I marched out of the room. I did not know what pushed my cruelty with Mori, but I was at the end of my rope. I ran my hand through my hair, careful to avoid the wax ears. All I wanted was her to come with me, to choose me over the Dragon Prince. I could not protect her, if she chose him over me, not even with this magic the dream man gave me. It came alive with my emotions; it consumed me when I thought of Morgana.

"I am here for Achilles," I said to the winged man at the livery. It dawned on me that he would expect extra payment. I had nothing to give him. I had nothing without Mori, but the tearing, searing pain of my soul. I loved her; she deserved to know. Every time I tried, she cut me off. It was what it was. I could not make her love me.

I allowed my head to clear of her and took a deep breath. It was then I took in my surroundings and chuckled. Why a livery in a world without horses? Now I had my answer. There were beasts, large horse like creatures from my world's mythology. The stalls overflowed with the Pegasus. Achilles was put to shame in his beauty, yet my charger still knew what these creatures could not. He knew battle; he knew of war and death. Most of all, he knew me.

A drumming sound, the tapping of fingers, brought my attention back. The stableman cleared his throat; I knew what he wanted. The man would surely listen to reason, or perhaps something of value remained in the saddle. Everything rushed through my head, as I conveyed the different situations and their conclusions.

"There are two emeralds for your troubles, good fine sir," Mori's serene voice lifted the weight off my shoulders. I watched her slink to the pedestal, and toss the jewels onto the registrar. The man smiled at his bounty. I could not care less. Morgana came to me; my princess chose me. Yet anger still radiated within me.

I coughed. "Milady."

She laced her arm through mine. I gave her a half bow, and gestured toward the walkway, but said nothing more. Together we walked to the rear of the stable. Achilles appeared delighted to see us and ready for the journey. His reigns were like home, worn and telling our tales. The leather was cool in my palm, as I led him outside. With one last look to the sky, I mounted my charger, and pulled the princess up. We rode out of Longawagon in growing and uneasy silence.

This was not how I envisioned things between us. There was a coldness rising in the princess, and it was not like her. Granted I only spent the last few days in her never-ending presence, but I assumed I witnessed the side she kept hidden away. I brought Achilles to an abrupt halt.

"Thomas, why do we stop?" I could hear the unpleasant irritation in her voice.

"Princess, we must speak before I shall allow my Achilles to take another step." Her reaction was indifferent, aloof. My hands flexed around the reigns. It frustrated me how easily she changed. Were all women this way, or just spoiled brats? No, I shook my head. Spoiled brats did not have to worry about their lives, they did not … God what was I thinking? Mori was the farthest from spoiled and bratty as one could be. How would I get through to her? If she went to the prince, she would not be free.

"There is nothing to say," she said. I watched the anger shoot to her hands, the green Myst forming, spreading out to me as if to grasp a hold. I prayed. Either this was punishment, or my true God could not hear the pleas in this world.

"Mori, please … I-" the darkness came to claim me before I could finish.

~~~

Oh no, what had I done? *No*, I cried out. It filled me with anger, with rage, and it got the better of me. The magic, the Myst attached itself to Thomas. No, poor Thomas ... I was not even angry with him. Something just snapped, as I left the inn. The giggles, the stares of the patrons, as I departed. I was not used to being exposed, and I took it out on the only one that mattered.

"What have I done? No, no, Thomas you must wake-up. You cannot leave me ... I love you too much. Gods, why have you forsaken me with such a curse? Let him live, let my love live," I pleaded, as tears streamed down my face. Achilles feeling my pain and anguish came to nudge its master. A small groan escaped from him, but his eyes remained shut. Thomas's heart beat rapidly, and his breathing became ragged. He was not going to make it.

I prayed the energy remained within me for another spell. *One more spell*, I pled to Freyr. I pulled upon the strength of the trees, grasses, and even the blanket of snow. More tears fell, as I began asking the elements for their permission, and pleading for their aid, before I released the magic within my heart. I blinked as the Myst rose from within the ground and me. The air, water, earth, and fire responded. The colors blended into a fine red haze. He breathed it in and his body glowed with the essence. The elements granted my wish.

They heeded my call out of love, my love for a human destined for death in this strange land. I, a member of the Unseelie court, Princess of the greater Alfheim Kingdom, scarred and broken, truly became the weakling my mother said I was. I fell in love with the enemy, the disgraceful humans who lived by the code of greed. Thomas proved different, or perhaps not all humans were as the tales spun around the fires and halls. Or maybe I just loved him for who he was.

"Surely, you did not grant him gifts just for me to take his life," I whispered knowing the Gods listened. A faint light of yellow mixed with my magic; it hummed louder with each passing second. Together we were stronger.

The energy flowed. It was then I noted the Myst did not return to the ground. The flow came back to me; the power moved me unlike anything else I ever felt before. Thomas coughed, and squinted at me. I expected him to become cross, to yell, to scream. Instead, he pulled me down, and kissed me.

A million bumbles battered around inside me, as his lips slowly parted mine. I had never kissed another before; was I doing it right? As if Thomas read my mind, he slowed his kiss even more, allowing me to feel every movement of his lips and tongue, as he explored my mouth. His warm whiskers tickled my skin, but it did not matter. Nothing would spoil the moment and my arms wrapped around his neck. A million years could pass, and I would not tire of this kiss. I wanted him to stay. Together, yes, we stood a chance. When he broke the kiss, a frown formed upon my face. Thomas cocked his head, and gave a smirk that somehow made him look more adorable, boy-like.

"It couldn't have been that bad, princess," he said, as he gazed around at the surroundings, before looking me in the eye.

"I didn't want you to stop."

He ran a palm over his face. "I love you, Morgana. Inside and out, I don't want you to marry the dragon … Hell; I don't want you to marry anyone." Thomas reached for me, but I stood up. I was unsure if I could give him what he asked for, was it as easy as saying no?

"Thomas, I love you too. I cannot promise you anything. I … my mother …" I said, as I sat back down, feeling weaker. He said nothing, pulling me into his arms, and kissing the top of my head.

~~~

I did not know what Mori or the human were thinking. It became clear that they were back on the run. I stopped, in Longawagon, in case anyone knew were they went. It took only a moment to put on my façade, and conjure items of value. Only the livery gave me any knowledge of use.

The crooked man, who held the emeralds I gave to Mori two weeks ago as a gift, told me the pair seemed at odds. He also pointed me to the south west, leading away from my lands. Just as I was about to depart, the man said one more thing.

"You seek the woman?" I nodded and jingled my pockets.

"They left not long before you arrived," the man repeated, and I grew impatient.

"The animal moves on foot, it has no wings." This I did not know about. No one had mentioned how they traveled. I assumed the man somehow held magic. Not far-fetched, as he was more than able to walk into our world.

"Did the woman seem in distress at all?" I asked the keeper.

"Not at first. They seemed rather odd from the start, whispering and such, and the man never drew down his cloak. Then today she looked as if she would murder him, a real coldness on her." That was all I needed to hear, before I was out the door. This human did something to my Mori. Never in the years I knew her, was she ever been able to achieve the emotionless, calculating persona. *That was her mother*.

I feared the worst, as I retook to the skies. The thought of her with the human pushed my will. They could not be more than half a day ahead, and that included the use of magic. Mori was magically inclined to say the least, but I could not rule out the human. There was an explanation behind his power to cross into my world. There must be another one to explain how he captured and used the princess to escape the fortress of Alfheim. I still refused to think that my Mori would do such a thing, not when we were close to marriage.

So caught up I had become, that I almost flew right over the pair. I hovered quite a distance away as to determine all aspects. Watching Mori proved the elf's words. It was as if ice ran through her veins. She unleashed that pain on the man. I watched him fall. Then just as I prepared to land, the princess screamed out, and rushed to the man's side. Tears fell, words of prayer left her lips, yet I still did not understand. I had to get a closer look, and watch this unfold, before I could fathom what happened.

The power Mori unleashed brought him down. But he too held Myst within his soul. I never witnessed a color such as the silvery yellow that flowed through him, in all the magic of the realms. This was new. I was both curious and intrigued.

Chapter Six
The Rise of the Myst

We knew the Prince of Dragons would hunt Morgana down. Just as we knew, her personal guard was a conniving, money hungry snitch. As Queen, it took only a jingle-jangle of persuasion to have him eating from my palms.

Word came in that the traitors stopped in Longawagon. It took a lick of magic to portal the guard to the location. To my dismay, they already departed. It was unfortunate, but I knew they could not be far from the town.

Within hours, both the Princess and the human would face my wrath. They would beg for leniency, but alas, I grew tired of this game. Mori was already becoming just another memory. Soon the kingdom would forget too, just as they forgot the rest of my daughters.

"Captain, how far till we catch up?" I asked over the beat of the Pegasus's wings. They could match even the fastest dragon in speed. The ground creature was no match for either.

"Not long, your Grace. I see Prince Drust going to ground." His eyes fell to the ground. "I suggest we do the same at the next passing, go the rest on foot. We keep the element of surprise that way."

"As you see fit Captain, we put this duty into your capable hands." It mattered little to me how we caught them, as long as we got them soon. Rumors spread and this was one I did not need.

Up ahead on the road, I caught sight of the black beast that vile man rode in upon days ago. The guards that captured them spoke of the calmness in the beast. It intrigued me; it had no wings, yet all other aspects would leave one to believe there was a relation to the Pegasus. The council decided to study the creature, breed it with our royal stock. The smaller size of the black beast could prove useful. Recapturing it now would set the lucrative plan in motion once again. The Unseelie court did not need the dragons to refill the coffers.

The King did not know how low the treasury dipped. The Kingdom of Unseelie ran dangerously low on both funds and supplies. The icy weather made for impossible growing and the majority of supplies came from the other kingdoms. A marriage to the Dragon Prince for Mori would have run us dry if not for the bargain; I struck the deal in secret with the dragon. His parents demanded a hefty dowry that the King could not pay. I went behind his back, asking Drust to front the ridiculous sum, with a promise to pay it back over time. He wanted her bad enough to pay it, and forgave the loan altogether.

After this fiasco, he may no longer want to take Morgana off my hands. That suited me just fine too. The girl would meet her demise, slowly and painfully after I killed the human. She would pay. I laughed and nodded. The prospect of torture seemed to lighten my mood, and now with Mori within my grasp there was nothing to stop me.

We began our decent from the low clouds. I saw both the Prince, and my daughter, though they remained apart. I blinked and chewed my lip. Mori was hovering over … leaning over the human.

"We ssshould ssstrike now while the human is down," the Captain Lotho hissed, and I gave my permission seeing the weakness. With magic, it was only a blink before we stood no more than 100 paces away. By then Morgana's lips were touching the human. My stomached curled. The sight sickened me, but they were wrong. The man was not harmed; he sat upon the cold, frozen ground with my daughter by choice.

I raised my finger in her direction. "Princess Morgana you are a fool and a traitor," the words dripping with my hate spilled from my mouth. There was no turning back or showing weakness now. Besides, Morgana was the weakest of them all and this, thing, was just a human. Still I expected her to jump, flinch, and any reaction that showed her as the coward. Mori did nothing of the sort; the man did not even look frightened. He grinned.

"My Queen." she bowed, but my daughter's eyes never left mine.

"Arrest them both," the Captain shouted, but as the guards moved in, I watched, as Morgana stood tall. There was an air about her. This human changed her. Myst billowed from her hands and feet. One, two, three, four, and a fifth element joined.

"On what charges, mother?" It was at that moment that I noticed the bruises, the cuts, and the scars vanished from her face. I blinked. The porcelain skin gleamed. Her beauty, even with her dark hair in tatters, was unparalleled to any in this world. It stunned me, yet it brewed the anger into my heart.

"Conspiracy to commit High Treason," I mumbled the charges, gritting my teeth in a rage. How dare she question me, and in front of these peasants. She had no right to challenge me. Morgana raised her hands up, palms facing the sky. The wind billowed her skirts and her eyes flashed. My heart beat a little faster.

"Then I charge you with the conspiracy to commit murder, acts against a nobleman, brutal force against your own crown." Her eyes bore into me, burning my skin. She clapped her hands overhead and lightening rippled through the grey clouds. I squinted; hail fell, pelting from the sky.

I could contain my Myst no longer. The long black tendrils shot forth. It sought Morgana, curling around her neck. Darkness they called it. I willed it to squeeze, to drain the life force from her body. A few more moments and I would have one less child to worry about. Mori smiled, ignoring the magic. The human grasped her hand and the fifth element spread over her body. Sizzled and popped, snapping against the Darkness. He lifted his free palm and aimed, willing his Light to consume me.

"Halt, Queen Magda of Alfheim, halt thisss inssstance, or you draw your lassst breath." The blade grazed my throat.

~~~

Upon witnessing the kiss, I knew whatever fell between the human and my Mori was real. I could lay claim to her no longer. It was then, right as I was about to depart, that my former guard and the Queen ported in. The bitter anger arose within me at the betrayal of my Captain scorched me. I planned to move on him first although the Queen remained the greatest threat. Stealthily I rounded back, and putting my finger to my lips, I alerted the guards to remain silent. There was no reason for them to doubt my duplicity.

The Queen and Morgana continued to exchange words and Myst. I noticed for the first time that her face bore no signs of injury. Everything faded away, but the internal scars would remain. If she had not shown me on a previous visit, I would have thought she lied. It was a shame. Though she was a great magnificence, the scars gave her an air of mystery.

The human stood by her side, and his palm shot forth magic. Like a worthy king, he was her equal, and proved as much. I believed his feelings for her rang true. Together, they were strong enough to overpower the daughter of Freyr.

Luckily, for me the Queen chose that time to begin her devious attack on Mori. I blinked, wondering if she lost her mind. All the previous attacks were secret. Few knew about that side of the Queen. It became clear she meant to take her daughter's life.

Even if that life was shared with another, I would not allow Mori pain, not like this. A day would come for her to end *Magda the Cruel*, as I called her. Today was not that day I brought the dagger to her neck and the Myst halted.

"Prince Drust, why have you drawn a weapon on me? Do you not see the games my daughter plays, the company she chose to keep? It was her, and her alone that freed this ... this man."

I laughed in her ear. "I know ... I know everything ... I mean everything ... your Grace. If ssshe diesss ssso ssshall you. Mori isss my friend. If the man isss hersss than he ssshall be mine. You will not harm her, not ever again ... my family will know the truth about the Unssseeliee courtsss."

I wished to see the look in her eye, as I slithered my words. Morgana may have hidden the emotions on her face, holding stoically, but her eyes were alight with the warmth I loved. That love was for the man now, until he departed our world.

"You will leave now, Queen of the unseely court. I sssuggest you return while it isss ssstill yoursss to claim." I walked over to the Princess Morgana and her human friend. Magda teleported out as I hoped she would. The princess and her companion would face her again, of that I had little doubt, but not today.

The guard Lotho stood frozen with fear. I would take care of him later. He would suffer and I would see to that myself. After all, I entrusted him with Morgana's safety, and he failed that task.

"Mori, my dearessst, you have had quite the adventure." She tilted her head and bowed to me.

The man did the same. His peculiar eyes stared me up and down.

"Prince Drust, this is Sir Thomas, and this is his horse Achilles." The horse made a sound and tossed his head. I smirked, and ran my hand over the sleek beast.

Thomas extended his hand and I took it. "It is a pleasure to meet you, Prince Durst. Mori has told me much about you." I noted his strange speech, but his demeanor showed me a man of honor. He shook my hand with vigor.

"I apologize if I gave you a fright. I had to know for myssself that Mori was sssafe. It ssseems ssshe is more than capable, asss are you." I cocked my head, noting the similar features we shared. Dark hair, strong build, but I towered over the man of light.

"Yes, I fear it still." His arm snaked around Mori's waist. "I am a warrior in my world, a Knight. We shield ourselves with faith, strength, and honor."

I smiled and rested a hand on his shoulder. "That is why you were chosen, Knight Thomasss. I have never witnessed thisss magic before. Doesss … doesss it have a name?" I asked. We were all a curious sort, but dragons grew bored. Shiny objects and magic held our interest the longest. Somehow, the man was both even if he no longer shined. I removed my hand, as my family called to me. I glanced to the sky and saw the messenger hovering. Magda summoned my court.

"The old man called me a paladin and protector of Alfheim. He told me to uphold my oath, to serve and protect," the Knight said, as he reached for Morgana's hand. The sentiment did not go unnoted.

"Freyr granted you the light. You must be very ssspecial to him. But it will not be enough to bring down the Queen. Magic to magic there isss one who can defeat her." My smile faded. Mori may not wish to hear what I had known all along.

"Who is that, Drust?" Morgana asked, with a light in her. Thomas made her stronger. In days, this mortal had brought her farther than her brother or me.

With him by her side, and I on the other, she would not fail. Mori gained much more than freedom if her mother perished or fled, and she knew the whole realm would fare better without the Queen.

"You milady." I watched the shock, form over her enlarging eyes. She knew nothing of her fate. The magic of dragons foretold these events. Not the exact events, such as the human, but we knew Mori would defeat her mother.

"Impossible, I barely have magic at all." I shook my head, but the human spoke, before I formed words.

"Mori, you healed me twice. Both those injuries should have killed me," Thomas told her, and I grinned. "Then the magic, the colored fog." Perhaps this human, as weak as he was, was the strength she needed.

"There is more power within you than you realize, Princessss. Ssshe wanted, nay needed you to be weak, and so ssshe grilled it into your head. At sssome point, you began to believe it. Now you have found your trigger. I sssuggest you learn to ussse it. Love, your love, will sssave usss all just at it repaired the damage her hatred wrought upon your face."

There were words that described the power she wielded. Morgana was a druidess, a shaman. Within her stirred the *völva*. The Myst was theirs to command, and it granted its power to those deemed worthy. She would not abuse it, and I prayed in time, she would help others on this path.

She blinked. "What?" My smile turned into a hearty laugh. No wonder she did not believe me.

"Your scars, the bruises, are all healed, my love," the Knight Thomas whispered into her ear, and I watched, as the pure glee poured out of her. I would always love her, but my love did not save the Princess Morgana.

~~~

Shock and awe had a way of painting the truth in life. I found it difficult to swallow Drust's words of truth. There was no argument that the Queen needed accountability for her actions. Even my father, the King should have done something to stop her.

"The others …" I could not find the strength to finish the sentence. My sisters …

"Perhapsss they truly lacked the power and ssstrength, Mori. It doesn't justify her actionsss, and you must make her pay." Drust took my hands in his, and away from Thomas who did not appear happy about it. But Drust was the gentle giant, who cared for me on some leviathan level. I was glad to have him as my friend.

"Is there nowhere safe for her to train … or grow her power, Prince Drust?" Thomas asked, as he slipped his arm about my waist, and pulled me closer. There was no jealousy in his voice, but the message to our dragon friend remained clear. My cheeks warmed at the barbaric exchange between the two.

"You need to train, Mori. One day you will train others too." He shifted his weight and glanced toward the sky again. "I cannot take you to my home asss I had wisssshed, not with your mother so clossse. We remain indifferent to humansss, young one, but there isss an alliance between the Unssseelie Court and usss. Your bessst bet is to head sssouth to your cousssin, Morgana. The Ssseelie Court is kind to humansss, and you are ssstill royalty."

Yes, but how long before the Queen sends out bounties and guards. I did not like the idea of relying solely on my power. In all my years, short as they were, it was inconsistent in the face of danger.

"What troubles you, Mori?" Thomas asked of me. My eyes fell to my hands. I did not see anything about me changed. At least not on the outside. "You are worried, my love," he whispered into my ear. "Stop chewing your lip."

My hand flew to my mouth and the Prince chuckled. My Knight knew me too well. How attentive, I thought, but alas, he was correct. Worried, I was, and I did not understand how to handle it.

"Drust,we are at least a week from the Seelie realm. Our rations are low, and the Queen will only send out hunters. I am pleased that I may be the one to stop her in the future, but I lack faith in my ability to protect us from danger now. At this rate we will starve or face attack before we leave the Unseelie border." A week by air, who knew how long the journey fared by land. There were three ways to traverse the distance. One, through the dragon lands, we could not risk. The second required a small boat. Yet I knew we could not leave Achilles behind. I had grown fond of him, as if he was my own, and I could never ask that of Thomas. That left one option, by land, and by way of the dwarven lands.

I stared, as Drust removed an item from his pocket. He infused it with a emerald light,. Before my eyes the scraps grew in size and resembled armor. Once finished he handed them to Thomas.

"Thessse items will be forged from magic. They will offer you protection, but asss a warrior, I am certain you know that you will not be invisible." Thomas took the pieces of brown leather and blackened dragon scale armor. He placed each piece on his body in a slow, fluid motion. Each one appeared to mold itself to him. It was not as flashy, as the metal armor, but something told me it was just as durable.

Drust held his hand up to signify that he was not through. From a satchel, he pulled a broad-sword, words etched into the blade, as he blew fire over the surface. The writing I recognized as Draconic. This in addition to the sheath, he handed to Thomas. The joy and sheer delight in his eyes made me want to celebrate.

"Morgana, I have a gift for you. This ssshould help to channel the myssst. It is a ssstaff of from great Ygg-drasil, and this cryssstal is a dragon's eye of the fiery flight. I hope it providesss the wisssdom and guidance you sssseek." I could find no words for such a powerful gift. Tears sprung in my eyes. The world tree reached through the Nine Realms, and formed the halls of the Bifrost. I threw my arms around him in a warm embrace.

"Thank you, Prince Drust." I stepped away as Thomas spoke. "I do not know how else to thank you," Thomas added with a bow.

"Indeed, we will be forever in your debt," I said, but he shook his head.

"Mori's happinessss is all the repayment I need … however, Knight Thomas, if you ssshould ever hurt the Princessss you will have to answer to me." Drust gave a wink and then he vanished before our eyes. Once again, we found ourselves alone. A woman, a man, and a horse. This time we had purpose and protection. More than anything, we had love, love for one another and the great understanding it brought.

"Are you ready to ride out, Mori?" Thomas pulled me closer, and kissed the top of my head. If it were at all possible, if the Queen was not a threat, I would have stayed there forever in his arms. My Knight, once in armor shining bright, would now become my paladin. A holy Knight, with a crusade to drive the dark evil from this realm. I would not allow him to fail.

"Yes, we must make it to the next village before nightfall," I said, realizing we may not make it.

"Why do you fear the evening so much?" Thomas asked, raising his brow..

"The Wisps, Thomas, they lead you astray. No creature has proven immune to their pull, but they only appear at night." The mere thought of them ran shivers up my spine.

"What are they?" He asked, as he lifted me atop of Achilles.

"They are the dead," I whispered, as eventide came upon us.

###

To Be Continued... Coming in 2014
Mayhem and Contention
A Nine Realms Tale
(Alfheim Two)

Fugitives Mori and Thomas, continue their journey into the vastly uncharted world of Alfheim. Abandoned by all, they only have each other for strength. With the Unseelie Queen hot on their trail, they must overcome the hurdles placed before them. The new couple begins questioning their force of contention and bonds of love, as they face continuous turmoil and mayhem; the pair embarks upon devious creatures and hopeless circumstances.

Sir Thomas struggles with his new abilities as a Paladin, and what it truly means to become a supernatural. Born of the mortal world, Alfheim and its inhabitants, test his bounds of faith and sanity. His only rock remains the princess who saved him from the gallows. With grand hopes of a happily ever after, the dream dissipates as a tumble nearly causes him his life. Everywhere he seeks guidance, danger and treachery lurks, waiting to claim his existence.

Princess Morgana remains torn between her love for Thomas and the love of her people. She fears that there isn't room for both in her life. If she can succeed in bringing down her mother, it will be up to her to reunite the Unseelie Court. Can the chaos driven inhabitants of her lands accept a Queen who loves, let alone a human for their King?

Coming January 2014
Tears of the Valkyrie
A Nine Realms Tale
(Midgard One)

About the Author

Rae Z. Ryans currently resides in Tumbleweed, Alabama, with her four demons (cats), three lycans (dogs), three sprites (kiddos), and her "normal" mood-shifting husband. She has lived all over the east coast and was born in Fairbanks, Alaska. Contrary to popular belief, Rae has never lived in an igloo.

She claims to be a socially awkward mouth breather who also owns a pink elephant that buy shoes. While there is plenty of proof that Rae loves shoes, no one has been able to prove the existence of Punky the elephant. She would point out that we can't disprove it either.

Rae is an alternate ego who enjoys writing urban and historical fantasy in her spare time. These works are often loosely inspired by Norse Mythology, but with plenty of unique twists. In real life she isn't very funny, and often comes off as sarcastic. In reality, Rae is down to earth and goes with the flow.

Rae often interacts with her fans, shares quotes, and asks for help in naming characters. In her words, "It is my utter downfall. I am filled with stories, but I lack the imagination to name anything."

www.raezryans.com
www.facebook.com/raezryans

Glossary of Terms

Abilities:
Shaman, Paladin, Warrior, Mage, Druid, Shape-shifter

Draco Queen:
Khazla Durkheim

Dwarven King:
Freaghard

Faerie Queen:
Gerd the Giantess, consort of Freyr.

Gods:
Freyr, Odin, Freya

Government:
Monarchy

Greater Faerie King:
Freyr, God of Light

Languages of Magic:
Old Norse

Mythical Creatures:
Wisps

Nine Realms:
Asgard, Alfheim, and Vanaheim make up the top tier, or upper realm.

Midgard, Jotunheim, and Svartalfheim make up the middle tier, known as Middle Earth.

Niflheim, Muspelheim, and Hel make up the Land of the Dead.

Pantheon:
Norse

Unseelie Queen:
Magda

Seelie Queen:
Selene

Races:
Elves, Faerie, Dragons, Dwarves

Realm:
Alfheim